Get your paws on all of the Puppy Powers books!

#1: A Wishbone Come True

#2: Wag, You're It!

Puppy Powers

Wag, You're It!

BY KRISTIN EARHART
ILLUSTRATED BY VIVIENNE TO

Scholastic Inc.

*To Ethan, who is a good sport, a great animal
companion, and a supercool cousin*

No part of this publication may be reproduced, stored in a
retrieval system, or transmitted in any form or by any means,
electronic, mechanical, photocopying, recording, or
otherwise, without written permission of the publisher. For
information regarding permission, write to Scholastic Inc.,
Attention: Permissions Department, 557 Broadway, New
York, NY 10012.

ISBN 978-0-545-61760-4

Text copyright © 2014 by Kristin Earhart
Cover and interior art copyright © 2014 by Scholastic Inc.

All rights reserved. Published by Scholastic Inc., 557 Broadway,
New York, NY 10012. SCHOLASTIC, PUPPY POWERS, and
associated logos are trademarks and/or registered trademarks
of Scholastic Inc.

12 11 10 9 8 7 6 5 4 3 2 1   14 15 16 17 18 19/0

Printed in the U.S.A.   40
First printing, June 2014

⭐ Chapter 1 ⭐

Max Harding ducked, scrambled, and threw. He looked to see if Lara or Miles was anywhere near where the ball would come down, but he couldn't see a thing. A mob of players from the other team ran down the field. The Buffalo players were all huge, and they blocked Max's view. All he could make out was the red of their jerseys.

A moment later, Max saw a red streak burst from the crowd. A kid with a buzz cut held the football high in the air. That was it. The game was over. It was another loss for Max's team, the Walruses. He guessed the Walruses were the worst team in the whole flag football league.

Lara and Miles ran over, along with the rest of the team. Max took off his jersey and knelt down to pet the coach's dog, a handsome husky named Hutch. Max only half listened to the post-game speech. Like always, the coach insisted that they had done their best and had fun. Coach said that was what it was all about. Then they all headed home.

Lara and Miles jogged to catch up with Max as he walked toward the other side of the park. "That was a good pass," Miles said. "I almost had it, but then one of the Buffalos batted it away."

"Sorry," Max replied.

"You don't need to apologize," Lara said. "We'll get them next week."

Max rolled his eyes. Unless they all magically grew six inches in seven days, Max was sure next week would be just like this one.

"Yeah," Max said, not wanting to hurt Lara's feelings. She always played hard. She never let the other teams get to her.

"This is our street," Miles said.

"See you on Monday," Lara added, and the twins waved before turning off.

Max cut across the grassy meadow. As he passed a group of older kids wearing yellow jerseys, they fell into pace next to him.

"Hey, it's our competition for next week," a kid with blond hair announced. Max recognized him from school. His name was Jason. He had been teammates with Max, Miles, and Lara last year. This season, he was on a different team.

"You guys are the smallest walruses of all time," Jason said. Max's head barely reached the other boys' shoulders. It was hard to believe they were in the same league. Jason and his teammates were all one or maybe two years older.

"Yeah, but I think the walrus is the perfect mascot for your team," one of Jason's friends added. "Because a walrus can't catch a ball, and you guys can't catch either."

Immediately, Max pictured a giant walrus lumbering around on a slab of ice, attempting to grasp a football in its floppy flippers. *Seriously. Who thought of the team names anyway?* Max wondered. The other mascots were fierce animals like bulls or wolves. Why did his team have to be a blubbery sea mammal?

The group of older boys fell silent but stuck with Max. Max wanted to say something back — something clever — but he knew it wouldn't fix anything. Still, he wanted to defend his team. They could catch and run good plays, just not against kids who were so much bigger.

Max wasn't scared of Jason or the other kids, but he didn't like the way they made him feel. He was relieved when they didn't follow him out of the park.

"The Bulldogs are all really scared to go up against the Walruses next week," Jason called as Max crossed the street. "Please don't scratch us with your long whiskers." Max could hear the other kids laughing. He imagined one of them slapping Jason on the back, congratulating him on a good joke.

Max was not looking forward to playing them. The Bulldogs. Max couldn't believe such a good name was wasted on Jason and his friends. Why couldn't Max's team have been some dog breed? Their coach had a husky. They should have been the Huskies.

Max loved dogs. He had always wanted one. His parents had talked about getting one a few years ago, but then he got a baby sister instead.

As he turned down his street he noticed his mom's minivan in the driveway, which meant she was back from the doctor. His little sister, Rina, had had a checkup. The car that his dad drove wasn't there. Max guessed that his dad and his big brother, Kazu, were still at the soccer tournament. Since his parents had been busy with his sister and brother, Max had been on his own that morning. He liked that, most of the time.

"Hey, Mom. Hey, Rina," Max said as he dropped his backpack on the floor and headed straight for the kitchen.

"Hey! How was your game?" Mom called from the other room.

"Fine," Max answered. He grabbed a granola bar and went back to the dinner table where Rina was finger painting. Their mom was next to her, chopping squash. Between them, the table was covered with paper, paints, books, and vegetables.

"How was your checkup?" Max asked Rina.

"Boo-boo," his little sister said, pointing to a purple Band-Aid.

Mom looked up. "It was from her shots," she said. "You were brave, weren't you, Rina?"

Rina nodded twice. She had just turned two and didn't say much, at least not much that Max could understand.

"Max, I didn't expect you home yet," Mom said, glancing at him as she sliced. "I thought you were volunteering today."

"I am, but I wanted to drop off my stuff. And get a snack," Max explained. He and his friends Lexi, Henry, and Sadie had just started volunteering at the local pet center. They were meeting there that afternoon.

"Okay, because your dad is planning to pick you up from Power's Pets later. He has a surprise for you," she said. She looked up at him. Dimples dotted her cheeks when she smiled.

"Yeah? What is it?" Max asked, hoping for a clue. He popped the last corner of granola bar in his mouth.

"I'm not telling," his mom answered, eyebrows raised. "But it's a good one."

★ Chapter 2 ★

Max half skipped out the door. A surprise! He couldn't remember the last time his parents had a surprise for him. They sometimes made a big deal about surprises for Rina, but she was only two. She got excited about a carrot.

Max tried not to think about the surprise, but he couldn't help it. He didn't want to be let down. He crossed his fingers and hoped it would be a puppy. Could it be?

He ran into his friend Lexi on the way. They walked the last few blocks to Power's

Pets together. She had Luna, her adorable black-and-brown pup, with her. As they walked along, Luna looked up at Lexi with kind, thoughtful eyes. Lexi had just adopted Luna that summer, but it seemed like they had been together forever.

Max thought about telling Lexi about the surprise, but he didn't want to jinx it. Still, he was curious.

"What was it like when you first got Luna?" he asked.

"It was great," Lexi answered. "I was kind of nervous at first," she added. "Mr. Power doesn't send the pets home with just anyone. The pet center works a lot like an animal shelter, so he has to approve the new owners first."

"He has to approve the owners?" Max questioned.

"He wants to make sure that the pet and owner are a good match," Lexi explained.

"It sounds complicated," Max said.

"Not really. Mr. Power just cares a lot about all the animals. There was only one puppy the day that I got Luna, but I would have known that she was the puppy for me, even if there had been a hundred there. Right, girl?" Lexi rubbed Luna's head, and the puppy yipped. "Why do you want to know anyway?" Lexi asked.

"Oh, just wondering," Max said. He hoped that she wouldn't ask him anything else. Luckily, he heard Henry and Sadie yelling to them.

"Hey, wait up!" Sadie's braids bounced behind her as she ran. Henry was on his scooter. Henry and Sadie greeted Luna with lots of petting.

"What do you think we're going to do today?" Henry asked.

"Whatever Mr. Power needs help with, I guess," answered Lexi.

"I hope we get to play with the animals," Sadie said. "I don't want to be stuck stacking bags of kitty litter."

"Um, remember last week?" Max asked. Just the week before, Mr. Power had asked them to design a new "amusement park" for the gerbil and guinea pig cages. He had all kinds of pieces they could put together. After they were done, they got to watch all the little fuzzy animals climb and spin and tunnel around.

"That was a blast," Henry said.

"Yeah," Max agreed. "I don't think Mr. Power will have us stack kitty litter anytime soon."

The four friends arrived at Power's Pets. As soon as they stepped inside, Max thought about what Lexi had said. It was obvious how much Mr. Power loved the animals there. They all seemed so happy and healthy. The large room echoed with cheerful chirps, squeaks, and yips.

"Hello?" Max called, looking around for Mr. Power. "Hello?"

The store grew unusually quiet. All at once, Max got the feeling that the animals were watching him. Gerbil eyes, kitten eyes, lizard eyes, all on him. Chance, the store dog, rushed up to him and pushed his chilly nose against Max's hand. Lucky, the store cat, usually sat back and watched the store, but not today. Today, Lucky trotted up to Max and wove herself between his legs. Next, the store parrot flapped off his bar and landed on Max's shoulder.

"Max is here! Max is here!" the parrot repeated.

"Wow!" Sadie exclaimed. "You're popular today. Did you wear perfume? Maybe a little Animal Aroma?"

"Um, I don't wear perfume," Max replied. He stood stiff, afraid to move. He had never had a giant bird on his shoulder before. It was cool, but he had a funny feeling something weird was going on. Chance sat by his side. Lucky continued to walk around his legs in a very sweet, reassuring way. She looked up at him, blinked her green eyes, and meowed.

"Well, hello!" a voice boomed from the back of the store. "I was wondering when you would arrive." Mr. Power clicked an old pocket watch shut and slipped it into one of the many pockets of his vest. "I was worried you weren't coming. And yet I knew you were."

The other three kids said hello. Max just nodded, his eyebrows creased together.

"Oh, my," the owner of the pet store said. "It looks like I'm not the only one who is glad to see you, Max." He chuckled. "Come along, Mango. Why don't you perch over here?" Mr. Power held out his arm and motioned to the bird.

Mango fluttered her green wings and flew over to Mr. Power. "Max is here," she announced again. Only the bottom of her beak moved when she spoke.

"The animals are all happy to see you," Mr. Power said, looking directly at Max. "Do you have some exciting news to share?"

Max stared at Mr. Power. Did the old man with the fishing vest know something about Max's surprise?

"Not really," Max said.

"Oh, well. The animals sometimes sense things," Mr. Power said. "They're clever that way."

Max looked down. Chance was still nudging Max's hand with his wet nose. Lucky blinked her bright green eyes again. Maybe they did know something, but what? Even Max didn't know what the surprise would be. After all, it was a surprise.

"I'm so glad you are all here," Mr. Power said to the friends. "We have twelve giant boxes of turtle food to unpack." He paused, looking from face to face. "I'm just kidding! Our kittens and puppies would love to play today. Sadie and Henry, how about you start in the kitty corner?" He pointed toward the front window. "Max, Lexi, and Luna, why don't you head over to the puppy pen?" He motioned to a large play area filled with cushions and toys. As soon as they got to the pen, the bell above the front door rang. "You kids go ahead. I'll be right back. I just need to help this customer."

Max nodded. Lexi grabbed Max's hand and started to tug him toward the puppies. That's when Max saw the customer who had come into the shop. The customer was Max's dad, and he was holding a brand-new collar and leash.

⭐ Chapter 3 ⭐

"Dad!" Max called, hurrying over. "You're early. I haven't even volunteered yet."

"Hey, Max," Mr. Harding said, putting his arm around Max's shoulder. "I wanted to make sure we had plenty of time."

"Time for what?" Max asked hopefully. He eyed the red collar in his dad's hand. Max could only think of one reason why his dad would have it.

Max's dad knelt down. Max could sense that everyone was watching: Mr. Power, Lexi, Henry, Sadie, and the animals. "So,

Max," Mr. Harding began. "Your mom and I have been thinking." Mr. Harding paused.

Why was his dad talking so slowly? Max couldn't take it! "Dad, what's that?" he asked, pointing to what his dad held in his hand.

"Well," his dad responded, "your grandparents sent it. It's a collar and leash. They wanted to give you something for your new dog."

"What?"

"They sent it all the way from Japan. They're really happy for you," his dad explained. Max's mom was Japanese, and his grandparents still lived in Japan. Max didn't see them very often, but they were always doing nice things for their grandkids. Buying the collar and leash was very nice, but that wasn't the real point. Max needed to make sure he truly understood what his dad was saying.

"You're telling me I can get a dog?" Max asked. His dad nodded. "But you and Mom said that our house is already all kinds of crazy."

"We did say that, didn't we?" Max's dad laughed to himself. "But we changed our minds. Your sister is older now, and we think a dog will be good for you. Besides, some families are just crazier than others."

Max's lip quivered a little. He was incredibly happy, so why did he want to cry? Max's dad pulled him into a big hug and patted his back. "Thank you," Max mumbled into his dad's shoulder.

Mr. Power and Max's friends had been trying to mind their own business. Lexi couldn't wait any longer.

"Come on, Max," she called from the puppy pen. "Don't you want to see the puppies?" Max smiled at his dad and they both headed over for a look.

"There are so many," Lexi told them, "and they are all supercute." Luna stuck her nose up to the pen and whimpered a friendly hello.

Mr. Power joined them. "I think I know which one you will choose," the owner of the pet store said.

Four puppies toddled over: a husky with crystal-blue eyes; a bulldog with lots of sweet, saggy wrinkles on his face; a sleek black mutt with pointed ears; and a tiny beagle who looked supersmart. Max just stared. Four perfect puppies, but which one was perfect for him?

Max had chills of excitement. He liked the idea of a husky or a bulldog. They were both tough, cool dogs, but he wasn't sure how to pick. Which one did Mr. Power think was right for him?

"So?" Lexi prodded.

"What do you think, Dad?" he asked.

"I think it's up to you," Mr. Harding said.

Max didn't say anything. He told himself he had to decide. Husky or bulldog? Just then, a fluffy golden retriever puppy crawled out of a cardboard box in the pen. The pup had a jolly grin and bright black eyes. Max thought he looked as cuddly as a teddy bear. If that puppy were his, he would call him Bear.

"So?" Mr. Power asked.

Max looked from the sweet golden retriever to the bulldog to the husky. "I like that one," Max said, pointing to the golden retriever.

"I thought you'd like Bear," Mr. Power said with a knowing smile.

Whoa! Max had guessed the puppy's name, without even trying. That was weird — spooky weird. Yes, Bear was a good match for the cuddly-looking pup. Still, there were lots of other good names, like Sonny, or Happy, or Salami Joe. But Max didn't think about the puppy's name because he was too overwhelmed by the actual puppy.

Mr. Power leaned over and lifted Bear out of the pen. "Want to hold him?" he asked.

Max held out his hands. As soon as Mr. Power let go, Max cradled the pup in his arms and pulled him close. He had that sweet puppy smell. Bear whined happily as he pushed his front paws against Max's chest and looked into the boy's face. The two made eye contact, and Bear broke out in a chorus of joyful yips. When Max laughed, Bear cozied up and started to lick his face. "Not my mouth, Bear," Max mumbled, trying to dodge the puppy's long tongue.

"Well, Bear likes you well enough," Mr. Power said, clasping his hands. "How do you feel about Bear?" Mr. Power looked at Max, then Max's dad.

"He's awesome," Max replied, trying to lift his chin so it was out of the puppy's reach.

"Awesome sounds about right," Mr. Harding agreed, tickling the puppy behind his ear. Bear started licking Mr. Harding's hand, too. First he licked Max, then his dad, then Max, then his dad.

"That's enough, big guy," Mr. Power said, taking Bear back into his arms. "You have plenty of time for licking, but first we have work to do. You too, Max. I need to show you Bear's special trick," Mr. Power explained. "Did Lexi tell you about Luna's trick?"

"Not exactly," Max replied. He looked around for Lexi, but she and Luna had wandered off to look at the fish. He noticed that his dad was filling out some paperwork.

"Well, Bear has a very special trick," the man said as he knelt down next to the puppy. "And you have to ask him to do it in a very special way."

Max sat down on the floor next to Mr. Power and the puppy. Bear was still so young. Could he really do a trick on command?

"Now watch," Mr. Power told Max before turning his attention to Bear. The puppy tilted his head to one side and gazed at Mr. Power. "Bear, sit," the man directed. The puppy tucked his back legs under him and sat down. "Good," Mr. Power said.

"Now wait, Bear." Mr. Power pushed his hand in a bag and pulled out a small orange circle.

"First you have to show him the treat," Mr. Power said. "Then place it on his nose." The man held the treat between his thumb and finger and carefully set it on the puppy's short snout. Bear watched Mr. Power closely and did not move. "Wait, Bear. Wait."

The puppy sat still, balancing the treat. He watched Mr. Power closely, his shiny black eyes filled with trust.

"Yes, good boy, Bear!" As soon as the puppy heard the word *yes*, he jerked his head back. The treat flew into the air and then dropped right into the puppy's open mouth. Bear wagged his tail as he chomped.

Max smiled and clapped. It was such a great trick that it took him a moment to notice a weird shimmer floating around the puppy. Blue and gold sparkles seemed to dance all around the room. Max turned to look for his dad and his friends. They had to see this! That's when he heard the voice.

"Don't worry about anyone else. It's time to focus on Bear and his trick. It's important you get it right."

Max looked around, trying to figure out where the voice was coming from.

Lexi was all the way on the other side of the store, and her voice didn't sound anything like that! The voice was deep and kind of gravelly, and it echoed in Max's head. It sounded like Mr. Power, but the older man's mouth wasn't moving. As soon as the voice stopped talking, there was a loud *POP*. The sparkles disappeared.

"You got that, Max?" Mr. Power asked in a kind, upbeat tone.

Max remembered what the voice had said, and he realized he needed to hear the directions again. "I'm sorry. Could you repeat the steps, so I can be sure?"

"Of course," the store owner said, scratching Bear behind the ears. He repeated the directions. "Does that make sense?" he asked when he was done.

Max nodded. "Yeah, I think so," he replied. The trick seemed very important to Mr. Power. Max wondered why.

Mr. Power gave Max a reassuring smile. "You and Bear will be great. You'll take good care of each other, I know."

When Mr. Power stood up and walked over to Mr. Harding, Henry and Sadie rushed to Max's side.

"He's so cute, Max!" Henry exclaimed. "Are you really getting that puppy?"

"I guess so," Max said as Bear climbed into his lap.

"Wow," said Sadie. "First Lexi, now you. Lucky!"

Henry and Sadie bent down to pet the content puppy. Max was content, too. He forgot all about the odd voice in his head. Nothing else really mattered, now that he had Bear.

⭐ Chapter 4 ⭐

"Thanks again, Dad," Max said as the two left the store. Bear was at their side, looking spiffy with his new red collar and leash. Mr. Harding had signed all the papers, and Max had his page of Puppy Pointers. It told him how to care for Bear. Even though he volunteered at the pet center, Max had not realized how much work a puppy would be. He wondered if his parents understood.

Max's friends followed them out of the store. They all waved good-bye. "I'm really happy for you, Max," Lexi said. Luna pricked her ears forward and added a cheery bark of congratulations.

Arf, arf! Bear replied.

Max waved back. He was really happy, too, at least until he saw Jason. The older boy was straight across the town square. He was playing ball with some friends in the grassy area by the school. His back was to them, but Max still knew it was the boy from the Bulldogs — the boy who used to be on his team.

Max gritted his teeth.

"I had to park in the school lot," Max's dad said. He pointed to the dark green station wagon.

"Come on, Bear," Max said. The puppy bounded along next to him. The clip on his leash jangled.

"You sure got yourself one happy pup," Max's dad said. "We'll have to send a picture to your grandparents. They'll like him."

Max was about to respond when a football came zooming toward them. Max quickly ducked and pulled Bear out of the way. Without losing stride, his dad reached up and snagged the ball from the air.

Jason jogged up. "Good catch," he said to Mr. Harding. "Thanks for getting it." Jason glanced over and seemed surprised to see Max. "Hi, Max," he said. Jason then looked down and seemed even more surprised to see Bear. "Oh, you have a dog."

"Yeah," Max said. "We just got him. His name is Bear."

"He doesn't look like a bear," Jason said with a laugh. "He's too small."

"How do you boys know each other?" Max's dad asked.

"We're in the same flag football league," Jason answered.

"Jason was on our team last year, but he switched to be with his friends," Max added. He didn't mention that Jason had been their quarterback, and now the Walruses didn't have a great passer.

"Yeah," Jason confirmed. "Our teams are actually playing each other next week. The Bulldogs better practice for the Walruses." Jason talked to Mr. Harding and didn't look at Max. "We might have to come up with some trick plays."

"Sports are a lot different than when I played," Max's dad said. "We just threw the ball after school. Pickup games, you know?" Mr. Harding tossed the ball back to Jason.

"Well, that was a great catch. You've still got the skills," Jason said, spinning the ball in his hand. He smiled without showing his teeth.

Max rolled his eyes. Bear, who had been sitting by Max's side, stood up and took a step toward Jason. He sniffed the older boy's leg.

"Hey, no," Jason muttered. He jerked away.

Grrruff, Bear barked. It wasn't the happy yip from earlier. This bark started with a growl. To Max, it sounded like a warning. Jason took several quick steps away. *Grrruff. Grrruff. Grrruff.* Bear stood his ground and barked.

"Man, you better learn to control your baby dog," Jason said, backing up farther. He passed the football from one hand to the other but kept an eye on Bear. "I'll see you at the game on Saturday, Max." He turned around and threw a long pass that soared through the air.

Max sighed with relief.

"I'm glad you're meeting new kids through football," his dad said. "I was surprised when you didn't want to go back to soccer this year."

"Yeah, well, that's Kazu's thing," Max replied. His big brother had been playing soccer since he was Rina's age, and he was good. Kazu was on his high-school team and a traveling team. Their parents were always driving him to practice or a game. Max just thought flag football was fun. At least it would be if his team could score.

"Well, I'll bet you're glad you stayed with football, now that you're quarterback. That's a big deal," Mr. Harding said, patting him on the shoulder.

Max didn't say anything. After Jason left the team, they needed a new quarterback.

When no one had volunteered, Max felt like it was his responsibility. He felt like he had to do it for the team.

"Well, Jason seems nice," his dad added. Max didn't have anything to say to that either. Jason was one of those kids who was good at being polite to parents. "But he's right. You are going to have to teach your puppy some manners."

Max frowned. That wasn't fair. Bear was just sharing how he felt. Max had read that a dog's bark could tell the owner how the dog was feeling. He wondered if Bear was trying to tell him something. "Bear's just getting used to us and being around new people," Max tried to explain. "He's a good dog. I can tell. And he can do a supercool trick."

Max reached down and lifted Bear into his arms. In less than a year, Bear would be almost as big as he was. It was hard to believe. But for now, the puppy snuggled up to his neck. Max got into the backseat of the car, still holding Bear. "I can show you our neighborhood," Max whispered as his dad started the car.

All the way home, Max pointed out the places he and Bear would go together. He showed the puppy Miles and Lara's street, the playground, and the bike path. Once, when Max wasn't paying attention, Bear licked his boy's face. The puppy wanted to celebrate all the fun yet to come.

When they arrived home, there was not a lot of time to fuss over the newest family member. Mom lifted Bear up, swung him around, and laughed out loud. (Bear smiled and wagged his tail.) Rina let Bear crawl all over her and got green finger paint on his blond belly fur. (Bear tried to lick the paint off her hands with his sloppy pink tongue, but Max stopped him.) Kazu put the pieces of his dirty uniform in the laundry to keep them away from the puppy. (Bear found the socks Kazu missed under the bed. He slobbered on them, but only a little. He was just trying to be helpful.)

But it was almost dinnertime, and everyone had a nightly chore to get ready. Dinner was special because it was the one time when everyone in the family was together. Bear was tired from the excitement of the day and crawled under the coffee table for a nap. Life was always busy at the Harding house. With Bear, it would be a little bit busier.

☆ Chapter 5 ☆

On Monday, it started to rain as Max raced home from school. He couldn't wait to see Bear. He was surprised when the puppy didn't meet him at the door.

"Hello?" Max called, hanging up his sweatshirt. "Bear?" A shrill scream was the only answer. It sounded like his sister. It sounded like his sister when she was very, very upset. "Rina?" Max called with concern.

Jolie, Rina's sitter, rushed into the family room with the little girl in her arms.

"She's been crying like this since she woke up from her nap," Jolie explained. "Do you know what she wants?"

Max looked at his sister's red face. Her orange T-shirt was drizzled with tears. Max shook his head. It was hard for him to understand Rina, even when she was speaking clearly.

A hiccup jolted Rina's tiny body, and more tears leaked out of her eyes. "Milk?" Max suggested, but Rina just cried louder.

Max heard a scratching sound and realized that Bear was in the backyard.

"He was chewing on all of Rina's toys," Jolie tried to explain, but Max was already heading for the back door. Lexi had warned Max that puppies like to chew on everything. They do it because they are teething, and because they want to investigate things.

Max took a deep breath and knelt down on the deck. Bear pounced onto his legs, with joyful whines. The puppy struggled to lick Max, aiming for his hands or face. He eventually just attacked Max's ankles. After a moment, he looked up at his special new friend and barked.

Max tried to figure out what kind of bark it might be. It wasn't the quick, playful yip from the pet center. It wasn't the lower, longer bark from meeting Jason. It was a bark that seemed to say that Bear wanted something. The puppy glanced in the family room window and whimpered. He looked into Max's eyes. *Arrf,* the puppy repeated.

"Are you hungry?" Max looked inside and could see the puppy's dish in the kitchen. It was still half full. "Do you want a treat?" Max asked.

Arf, arf!

Max was certain that was it. "I'll give you a treat if you do your special trick."

Arf, arf!

Max pulled a bag of treats from his pocket. He'd only had a dog for a couple days, and he already had his goodie bag at the ready. "See the treat, Bear?" Max placed the treat flat on the puppy's nose. "Wait, Bear," he directed. Max locked eyes with the puppy and counted to five. He could see the ring of white around the shiny black of Bear's eyes. It made Bear look very wise. "Yes, Bear. Good boy!" Max exclaimed.

At once, the puppy gave his nose a jerk, and the treat flipped into the air before falling into his mouth.

Max laughed out loud. He reached forward and scratched the puppy around the neck. It took him a moment to realize that the air was once again filled with sparkles, and he could hear a voice in his head. He was certain it was his sister. "*No milk. Water,*" the voice said. "*Water and new buddy eggplant.*"

"Rina?" Max said, looking around.

"*Water and new buddy eggplant,*" the voice said again. Max could not see his little sister anywhere, but he couldn't really see that much with all the sparkles swirling around. "*Water and new buddy eggplant,*" the voice repeated, and then there was a *POP*!

Max wasn't sure what had happened, but he was sure that he had to find his sister. He gave Bear a pat on the head. "You can come in with me, but you have to leave Rina's toys alone. Okay?" He picked up the pup in one arm and opened the door with the other.

Inside, Max could still hear Rina hiccupping between cries. "Rina? Jolie?" he called. He didn't know how he had heard his little sister when he was all the way on the deck, but it had sounded like her. The babysitter appeared in the kitchen doorway. Max thought she looked tired. She was holding a sippy cup full of milk. Rina peeked out from the doorway, sucking on her Binky.

"I was thinking," Max began, "that she might want water."

"Water?" Jolie asked.

"Yeah, she sometimes likes that instead of milk," Max said. "And I'm going to her bedroom to look for her new toy."

"Thanks," Jolie said. "And you'll keep track of that cute dog?"

"Yes, I will," Max said, giving Bear a

squeeze. "No chewing," he said, tapping Bear on the nose.

Still holding the puppy, Max ran upstairs. He went into Rina's room. His grandparents had sent Rina a silly stuffed eggplant toy, and she loved it. The eggplant was not in her toddler bed. Max looked at the toy box, which was overflowing "If I put you down, will you be good?" Max asked. Bear seemed to smile as he gave a yip.

Max put Bear on the floor and started searching. The toy box contained enough animals to fill a zoo, but there was no eggplant. It wasn't until Max was done looking in the closet that he realized Bear was gone.

He heard barks coming from his parents' room. *Oh, no*, he thought. What if Bear had gotten ahold of one of his dad's work shirts or his mom's good shoes? Max ran into the room. He couldn't see Bear, but he could see something scrambling under the covers on the bed. "Bear!" he yelled. "You promised!"

The puppy growled playfully and backed out from under the comforter, rump first. When he turned around, there was a fuzzy purple eggplant hanging from his mouth.

"Oh, Bear, you didn't get it too wet, did you? Let go," Max demanded. He smoothed the covers. The puppy dropped the eggplant

in front of Max and wagged his tail. "Good boy" was all that Max could say.

At dinner that night, Max's mom told his dad the story. "Jolie was so grateful. She said it was as if Max could read Rina's mind."

"It wasn't me," Max insisted. "It was Bear. He's the one who found the eggplant."

"Buddy," Rina said between bites of noodles.

"Yes, Buddy. That's what you named your new eggplant, isn't it?" Mr. Harding said.

Rina nodded.

"Max, we appreciate you helping Jolie and Rina. It's how we make things work in this family," his mom said. She smiled at him.

Max still wasn't sure what had happened that afternoon. How could he have heard Rina so clearly when he was all the way outside? He was trying to figure that out when he heard his dad make an announcement.

"We should all go to Max's football game this weekend," Mr. Harding said. "He's playing quarterback." Their dad pointed his chopsticks as he talked. He always started with chopsticks when they had noodles. Then he usually switched to a fork and spoon halfway through.

"That sounds good. We can take a picnic," their mom said. "It'll be fun."

"I don't know how fun it will be," Max mumbled, swirling his noodles in the broth. Adults always made a big deal about how sports should be fun.

"What was that, honey?" his mom asked. "Aren't the Walruses doing well this season?"

Max sighed. How could he explain everything that was wrong with his team? "I just wish we weren't the Walruses. Some kids were making fun of us. They were saying that walruses aren't tough enough. I want a cooler mascot."

"If you want something more intense, how about the Walloping Walruses?" Kazu asked, making himself laugh.

Mr. Harding laughed, too.

"Well, I've read that walruses can be downright fierce," his mom said. "The mothers will do anything to protect their little walrus cubs, so I think it's a great team name. Besides, walruses can pull themselves out of the water with their tusks. That's cool."

Max gave a small smile. His mom was funny. He had no idea why she thought those walrus facts would be helpful, but it was nice that she was trying.

"Walloping Walruses," Kazu repeated, pumping his fist in the air. Mr. Harding cracked up again. This time, Max had to laugh, too.

⭐ Chapter 6 ⭐

Before school the next day, Max and Kazu picked up anything that Bear might try to chew. The puppy was napping in his crate, so it was a good time. Otherwise, Bear would have challenged them to a game of tug-of-war over every single sock and shoe.

"I don't see why I have to pick up when it's your puppy," Kazu complained, leaning over to grab a napkin from under the table. Kazu wasn't much for picking up. The only thing that was neat in his room was the shelf of soccer trophies.

"He's not only mine," Max explained. "Bear is the family dog. I just promised to do most of the work." He really did want Bear to belong to the whole family. It would be more fun that way.

"Well, Rina leaves toys lying around all day long. We can't do anything about that," Kazu said, motioning to all the plastic play food on the floor. "She's worse than I am."

"But she's two," Max insisted, putting the remote on the TV stand. "And you're fourteen!"

"Yeah, well, she should still do her part," Kazu complained, but Max knew his big brother was kidding.

Max was in a good mood all the way to school. He was thinking about Bear's playful growl when someone bumped into him. It was Jason.

"Sorry, dude," Jason said. A smile played at the corners of his mouth. "I was just thinking about your cute little dog and your cute little football team."

"Yeah?" Max said. "That's kind of weird. I guarantee my dog and my team-mates were not thinking about you." Max immediately regretted his response. Why did he have to make a joke?

"Well, maybe the Walruses should start thinking about me and the other Bulldogs, because we are going to beat you on Saturday. You won't know what hit your blubbery little walrus bodies."

Max wanted to point out that they were

playing flag football, so tackling was not allowed. But he didn't say that. He knew a clever reply could backfire. "Well, my mom told me that walrus blubber can be over three inches thick, so that's pretty good protection." *Oh, brother.* Max rolled his eyes at himself. Why was he quoting his mom's crazy animal facts?

"Your mom told you?" Jason asked. "You're a sweet kid, Max, but it won't do you any good on Saturday. There's no way you'll win. No way." When Jason patted Max on the shoulder, it didn't hurt, but it stung. Why had Max decided to play flag football anyway?

"Were you just talking to Jason Strait?" Lara asked. Miles, her twin, was right behind her. The three teammates watched as the older kid strode away down the middle of the hall.

"Yeah, I guess so," Max said. "He was warning me about our game on Saturday.

He knows that the Walruses don't exactly have a quarterback."

"Ugh. We play the Bulldogs this weekend?" Miles grumbled. "Maybe I'll be sick."

"You can't be sick," Lara insisted. "You'll be at the park if I have to drag you with one hand and hold a barf bag in the other."

"Yuck," said Max.

"What?" Lara said with a shrug. "We're twins. We're close."

"Maybe too close," Miles replied.

That afternoon, Max decided to take Bear for a walk. He had been thinking about the day before. How had he heard Rina when he had been outside with the door closed? Max thought that the voice had come from inside his own head — just like at Power's Pets. Max had a theory. Bear was part of that theory, and Max wanted to try it out.

Bear was excited to be outside in the crisp fall air. Every few steps, he jumped up on Max's leg, getting caught in the leash. "Bear, I need to teach you better manners," Max said, lifting up the puppy's paw and shortening the lead.

When they finally reached the park, Max looked for a good place to test his theory. It didn't really matter where, but he needed for people to be close by. Max passed the playground because it was too loud and crowded. He wouldn't be able to hear himself think.

At the edge of the meadow he could see Lara and some of her friends playing football. He watched as Lara took the ball and looked for someone to throw to. She let the ball go, and it sped through the air. The girl she had thrown to couldn't run fast enough. It went over her head and landed near Max.

Nice throw, Lara! Max thought. Max

hoped she wouldn't decide to switch football teams next year, like Jason.

"Let's get the ball," he said to Bear.

He led Bear over to where the ball had landed in a pile of leaves. The girl who had missed the catch came closer, and Max realized it was Sadie.

"You brought Bear!" Sadie leaned down and immediately started rubbing Bear's ears. The puppy loved it. "It's Max!" Sadie yelled to the rest of the group. "He has the cutest puppy!"

The group started running and had soon surrounded them. Max gave Lara the ball and then introduced everyone to Bear. The girls had lots of questions for Max. They all tried to pet Bear at the same time.

"Does he do any tricks?" Lara asked.

Max nodded. It was time to test his theory. "Watch this," Max said.

"Bear, I need you to pay attention," Max started. He showed the puppy the treat. As soon as Bear had his eyes fixed on the treat, Max set it on his nose. "Wait, Bear, wait," Max directed. Bear looked longingly at the treat. Then his eyes wandered to the faces of the girls in the crowd. Then he looked off in the distance.

"That's adorable," they cooed.

After enough time had passed, Max praised the puppy. "Yes! Good boy, Bear!"

Bear tilted his head back so the treat went into the air. He followed the treat with his eyes and then gulped it down, licking the edges of his tiny jaw.

Sure enough, Max soon saw the sparkles floating around Bear. Next he noticed that the sounds of the girls clapping and talking were muffled. Then he heard a single voice in his head. It said, "*I wish someone would offer to watch my cart. I need to go to the bathroom.*"

POP!

⭐ Chapter 7 ⭐

What? That was not what Max had expected. He had expected to hear the voice of one of the girls, but this hadn't been anyone familiar. This voice was deep and gruff. The sparkles were gone. Max didn't hear the voice anymore. He could only hear the girls talking about Bear.

"He really does look like a teddy bear when he sits like that," the girl standing next to Lara said.

"He's so cuddly," added another.

Max looked at Bear. The puppy was

staring off into the distance again. Max followed the puppy's gaze. He saw a man with an ice cream cart at the edge of the playground. His parents had bought him cones there lots of times. The voice had definitely belonged to a man, and that man had said something about "his cart." Max decided it had been the ice cream man. He guessed that the ice cream man must really need a restroom break.

"I'm going to get some ice cream," Max said.

"Isn't it close to dinnertime?" Sadie asked, her eyebrows raised.

Max glanced at his watch. It was getting late, and his parents were kind of strict about being home for dinner. It was the one thing they made a big deal about. "I'll just see what flavors they have," he said as he gave the leash a pull.

"One more round before we go home?" Lara asked the group. They all nodded.

"We'll see you later, Max," Lara called. "Bye, Bear!" Some of the girls in the group said good-bye to Max. They all said bye to Bear.

Max hurried across the grass toward the cart with the umbrella. Bear loped along beside him. The ice cream man was standing with his hands in his jacket pockets, watching the playground. Max didn't know what to say.

"Um, do you want to take a break? Maybe go to the bathroom?" he asked. "I can watch your cart."

The man looked hard at Max. "I know you, don't I?" He tilted his head at Max.

"Yeah, I'm Max. I've gotten your ice cream lots of times," he said.

"Well, I'm Michael," he said. "I really appreciate you and your guard dog watching the cart." He patted Bear on the head before walking away.

Max sat down on a park bench to wait.

It took Bear three tries to jump up next to him. Then the puppy sat down next to his boy. Max scratched him behind the ear. "That's a pretty special trick, Bear, that whole catch-the-treat-out-of-the-air thing you do." Max didn't know how, but it seemed like he could hear someone's thoughts every time Bear did his trick. Pretty weird. He remembered how important the trick was to Mr. Power. He remembered the sparkles. It didn't seem possible, but there was only one explanation. The trick had to be magic.

Max heard a rustling and looked up. There, high on a tree branch, sat a black cat with white whiskers. "Lucky?" he asked. "Is that you?"

Max thought it looked just like the cat from the pet center. Then, when the cat winked at him with one of her sparkly green eyes, Max was sure.

Bear started yipping. He jumped up on Max's leg and barked.

"What's going on, boy?" Max asked. "Why are you so excited?" Something told Max that Bear really wanted to do his trick. "Do you want a treat, boy?"

Arf! Arf! The long fur on the puppy's ears flopped as he scampered around on the bench.

"Okay, okay," Max said. Bear sat down without being asked, and Max placed a treat on the blond stubble just behind the puppy's coal-black nose. Bear waited, his tail thumping on the planks of the bench.

"Yes, good boy, Bear," Max said. Bear tossed the treat and snapped it out of the air. This time, Max knew to expect the sparkles. He also knew that he couldn't guess whose voice it would be. There were kids on the playground, joggers passing by, and a group of old men playing horse-shoes. When Max did hear the voice — with the odd echo in his head — it was a voice that he thought sounded familiar.

"Oh, no. There's that dog again. No way do I want to go anywhere near that dog. I don't trust it. I'm not even getting close. No way."

POP!

Max looked around. The puppy had been watching the playground, but now he turned back to Max. Was he trying to tell Max something?

All the times before, the thoughts seemed to share good information — in Power's Pets, with Rina, and in order to give Michael a bathroom break. This time, Max couldn't figure out whose thoughts he had heard or what they meant. The voice sounded like a kid, definitely a boy. And, from what the voice said, Max was pretty sure the boy was afraid of dogs.

"That guy should meet you, Bear," Max said. "No one would be afraid of a good pup like you." Max had read a lot about dogs since getting Bear. He knew that dogs could sense a person's fear. Sometimes a dog reacted by growling or barking. If a dog did that, it might make the person more afraid. "Too bad we don't know who that guy is," Max said as he pet one of the dog's silky ears.

Michael, the ice cream cart owner,

came back. He gave Max a free cone, which Max shared with Bear.

Max had been so lost in his thoughts — and his ice cream — he forgot to check the time. "Oh, no, Bear," he said. "We have to run." And he meant it.

Max took off, and the puppy jogged next to him at first. Max stopped at the edge of the park and waited to cross the street. When the light changed, Max started to sprint across, but Bear stayed put. "Come on," Max said, tugging on the leash. Bear stood up and trotted forward, but his stride was short. His tongue drooped out of his mouth.

"Oh, man!" Max grumbled when they got to the end of his block. Even in the dusk, Max recognized the kid in the dark blue warm-up jacket. It was Jason, and he was with one of his friends who lived on Max's street. The last thing Max wanted was to run into Jason.

Bear looked too tired to walk any farther. Max knew the puppy would never make it the long way around the block. With a huff, Max lifted Bear and started walking as fast as he could. When he had looped around and arrived at the other end of his street, he ran into Lexi.

"Hey, Max," she greeted him. "Luna and I are just finishing our evening walk." Max noted that Luna was growing taller and leaner, no longer a roly-poly pup.

"Oh, Bear and I are just heading home for dinner." Bear snuffled up against Max's sleeve, his eyes nearly closed.

"Dinner? Your family eats late," Lexi said.

Max guessed his family had already started eating. They had to be wondering where he was.

"I'll walk you home," Lexi suggested.

Max nodded. By the time they reached Max's mailbox, the older kids were gone. "Well, have a good dinner," Lexi said as she led Luna away.

"Yeah," Max said under his breath. But looking at his watch, he was pretty sure there wasn't much of a chance for that.

✯ Chapter 8 ✯

Max's parents weren't angry — at least not right away. At first, they were relieved. They both got up from the table and rushed to meet Max at the door. "We were about to go out and find you," his mom said.

"We're so glad you are all right," his dad said, placing a hand on Max's shoulder. His mom smothered him and Bear with a giant hug.

Max had only been fifteen minutes late, but no one was ever late for dinner at the Harding house.

Max made sure Bear had food and water before joining his family at the table. Bear drank an entire bowl of water. Then he headed straight for his crate and fell fast asleep.

Max's parents let Rina and Kazu finish talking about their days. Then they asked Max the hard questions. Max didn't know how to answer them. *Why did he offer to watch the ice cream guy's cart? Why didn't he take the fastest route home?*

"I'm sorry," Max said several times, and he meant it. He felt bad.

He felt worse when his parents wondered if Bear was too big of a responsibility for Max.

"Maybe it is too much for you right now," his mom said.

"We'll give you another chance, Max, but you have to prove you're responsible enough," his dad advised.

Max nodded and looked over to where his puppy was sleeping. Bear was really worn out. Max had pushed him too far. He promised himself he wouldn't do it again.

The next day, Max came straight home after school. He grabbed a banana and Bear's brush. Then he took Bear to the backyard.

"No walks today, Bear," he said. His only plan was to brush the tangles out of the puppy's tail, but it wasn't easy. Bear's tail would not stop wagging. "No tricks either." Max suspected that Bear had done his trick too many times. That might have been why the puppy had been so tired. "We're going to take it easy."

The puppy gave a lighthearted yip and lay down next to Max. He rolled over, so Max could brush the soft, wavy fur on his belly. *Arf,* he barked again.

"Hey, champ. Hey, Bear."

Max looked up and saw his dad closing the back door.

"You're home early." Max said it almost like a question, doubting it was true.

"Yeah," Mr. Harding said. "I thought maybe you'd want to throw the ball or something." He already had the football. He tossed it up with a spin and caught it again.

"Sure!" Max gave Bear one last brush and stood up. He remembered how Kazu and their dad had often played soccer, before Kazu had practice all the time.

Max headed to one side of the yard, clearing Rina's plastic shovel and pail out of the way as he went. His dad threw a straight, spiral pass as soon as Max had turned around.

"Max," his dad said just before catching a pass, "I feel bad about yesterday. I know you understand that dinnertime is important." He threw the ball back Max's way. Max caught it easily. "And I know adding a puppy into the mix complicates things. We don't want you to feel like you have to do it all alone." He caught Max's pass and held the ball in both hands. "We're a family, so you've always got us. We can help with Bear when you need us to."

Max nodded. "Got it," he said. "Thanks." Max paused a moment and then threw the ball back. "I might need help with Bear sometime. But I really need help with my football. We're playing a tough team Saturday, and I'm kind of nervous." Max wasn't sure if he was nervous about playing the Bulldogs, or seeing Jason.

"What's the problem?" his dad asked. "You're throwing and catching well."

"I don't know," Max replied. "The other teams are bigger. They always grab our flags before we get anywhere." That was one of the major problems. In flag football, the play was over as soon as someone grabbed the flag from a player's belt. "Their arms are so long, they're like elasto-men."

His dad laughed. "You've got to get past the size thing. There are good things about being small. Bigger isn't always better."

"I guess," Max mumbled. "I just don't want to let you guys down. You know, with the whole family being there."

"No way. You can't think about it like that, Max. It's not about winning. Just help your team play its best," his dad said, "and there's no way I won't be proud."

Max looked at the ground and let his dad's words sink in.

After a moment, his dad said, "Now go long." Max looked up as his dad got ready to pass. He took off running. He glanced up over his shoulder, and the ball dropped safely into his hands. If only the games were as easy as that.

★   ★   ★

That night, Max was still thinking about what his dad had said. One phrase kept replaying in his head. *There's no way I won't be proud. No way . . .* It was very reassuring, but it also reminded Max of something else.

It reminded him of Jason. Jason always said "no way." The voice Max had overheard in the park had said it, too. *There's no way I'm going near that dog. No way.*

Max thought about it. He remembered how Bear had barked when he first met Jason. And how Jason had quickly backed away. Could Bear have picked up on something? Had Bear barked because he sensed Jason was afraid? Max couldn't be sure. The one thing he did know was that he had one special puppy. So far, it seemed like Bear's magic had the power to help people, and it was Max's job to figure out how.

★ Chapter 9 ★

"Go get 'em, Walloping Walruses!" Kazu called, giving Max a light slap on his back. "Have fun."

Their mom smiled from her spot on the large, plaid picnic blanket. Rina was blowing bubbles. She didn't know the difference between a football and a soccer ball . . . yet. Max's dad was standing, surveying the field. Bear's leash was in his hand. The pup had been spunky all morning, wagging his whole back end.

"I'll be back, boy," Max said, giving his puppy a hearty back scratch. "Root for the Walruses!"

Max waved when he saw Miles and Lara headed his way. There was a group of tall boys with yellow jerseys not far behind them. Max shook his head. His team really was small.

In the huddle before the game, he could tell his teammates were worried, too. "No wonder Jason Strait changed teams," one kid said. "The Bulldogs look like they could play in the pros."

"My dad said bigger isn't always better," Max said. "And it's true. We're small and fast. We can get right up next to them and grab their flags." The team seemed to take in his words.

"That's a good can-do attitude," Coach chimed in. "Don't worry about how big they are. Just grab those flags!" The coach led a group cheer, and the team hit the field.

Halftime came before anyone knew it. Neither team had scored. "Nice call, Max," Coach said during a water break. "You guys are small and scrappy. You just keep grabbing those flags and we have a chance." The Walrus players had been scampering around and ducking under the bigger guys to snatch the Bulldogs' flags. It kept the other team from getting points, but the Walruses didn't have any points either.

Max felt like scoring points was his job. He was quarterback. Like his dad said, he had to figure out how to do what was best for the team.

It didn't take long for the Bulldogs to score in the second half. Of course Jason threw their one touchdown pass. Max wasn't sure his team would ever make it to the end zone.

Somehow the Walruses kept the Bulldogs from making any more big plays, but time was running out. Max was exhausted. He had been running all over the field but had not completed a pass. Every time he got the ball and saw the other team rushing toward him, he froze.

He was trying to figure out a new plan as he ran back on the field. He could hear his mom cheering. Max searched for the blanket where his family was sitting. First he saw his mom. Then he saw his dad. His dad was putting a treat on Bear's nose.

Almost immediately, things became blurry. The air shimmered, and Max saw blue and gold sparkles. "What?" Max mumbled. "No, not now!" He had to call a play. That's when he heard the voice.

"We don't have much time to win this thing. If I were Max, I'd tell everyone to run deep. Then I would throw the ball as far as I could. It's our best chance to win."

POP!

"Come on, Max," Lara said. The whole team was staring at him. They were all in the huddle, waiting. "We need you to call a play."

Max thought about what the voice in his head had said. He knew he had to do what was best for the team. He made a decision.

"No," Max said, "I'm not calling a play. You are." He handed the ball to Lara. The voice he had heard was clearly Lara's. She knew what play she would call if she were quarterback. Max wanted to give her the chance.

"But I've never played quarterback before," Lara insisted.

"Yes, you have. In the park," Max replied. "And if you think about it, I bet you know exactly what play you would call to win the game."

"Hurry up!" a player from the Bulldogs called.

"What's taking so long, Walruses?" Jason yelled.

Lara took a deep breath and looked at her teammates each in turn. "Okay, I need all the receivers to go long. I'll throw it as far as I can."

"Sounds like a good plan," Miles said, clapping his sister on the shoulder.

"And Max," Lara said. "You should go long, too."

Max nodded, and the team got in position for the play.

When Max lined up, he was right across from Jason. He avoided the other boy's eyes. He tried to think about running toward the end zone.

The whistle blew. Max needed to get downfield. He might not be quarterback, but his team still needed him. He dodged one player and then another. He ran toward the other end of the field. He turned just in time to see the football hurtling at him. He reached up and grabbed it with both hands and ran.

The next thing Max knew, the Walruses were all in the end zone, jumping up and down. They had scored a touchdown, their first of the season.

The game ended in a tie. In his post-game speech, Coach congratulated Lara on her amazing throw. "You have an arm like a cannon," he exclaimed. "I don't know how you ended up throwing the ball, but I hope you do it again next week."

Lara grinned.

"And Max made a fantastic catch," Coach added. "You all did your part, and you played like a real team. I'm really proud."

★ ★ ★

When Max got to the picnic blanket, Kazu gave him a high five. His mom gave him a hug. "Way to go, champ," his dad said.

Mr. Harding gave Bear's leash to Max and started to fold the picnic blanket.

Bear yipped a greeting. Then he yipped again and again.

"What is it, boy?" Max asked. He knew Bear was trying to tell him something. Max looked around. He saw Mr. Power sitting on a park bench, petting Chance. The old man looked up and tipped his cap to Max. Max waved.

"Is that what you wanted me to see?" he asked Bear. But when Max turned back, his puppy was looking at something else: Jason. Bear was watching the other boy as he walked past.

Max decided this was his chance. If Bear's magic had helped him figure out that Jason was afraid of dogs, then Max wanted to try to do something about it.

"Hey, Jason," Max called out. "Good game."

Jason hesitated, looking first at Max, then at Bear. Bear was tugging at his leash, wagging his tail, and pulling toward the other boy.

"I think Bear wants to say hi," Max said.

Jason looked at him, eyes wide. "No way, dude," he said.

"Maybe just let him smell your hand?" Max suggested.

Jason looked around the park.

Max bent down and stroked Bear's back. "It's okay, Bear. This is Jason." Bear looked up at the other boy and whined hopefully.

"Okay," the older boy said, almost swallowing the word. Jason knelt down and held out his hand. Bear stepped forward and gave it a sniff. He looked back at Max.

"That's a good boy, Bear," Max said.

After another sniff, Bear licked Jason's hand. At first his tongue barely touched the boy's fingertips, but then Bear wiped his wet tongue between Jason's fingers and on both sides of his hand.

"It tickles," Jason said, making a face.

"I know," Max agreed. "You get used to it."

"Yeah, I guess so," Jason said, standing up and wiping his hand on his pants. "Your dog's pretty nice — and you played a good game today, too."

Somehow, Max knew he meant it. "Thanks," he said. "I think we kind of surprised ourselves. I'll bet Lara is our quarterback from now on."

"Sure. She was good." Jason put his hands in his pockets and gazed around the park again.

"Hey, Max!" Kazu called. "We're leaving." Kazu motioned for his brother to follow.

"Well, I gotta go," Max said.

"Me too. See you at school," Jason said, heading off. He turned back around when he was a few steps away. "I guess Walruses can catch after all."

Max couldn't think of anything clever to say. He just laughed. Then he ran to catch up with his family. Bear loped along beside him.

Max fell in stride next to his dad. "That was a real showdown out there," Mr. Harding said. "The Walruses looked good."

"Yeah, we didn't wallop anyone," Max said, "but we did have fun."

"And that's what it's all about," Kazu and Max's dad said at the same time.

Max laughed. If this was what it felt like to tie a game, he couldn't imagine what it felt like to win.

As if reading Max's mind, Bear gave a loud, happy bark. Max smiled at his puppy, and his puppy smiled right back.